W0009913

The Tin Soldier

Based on the story by
Hans Christian Andersen

Retold by Russell Punter

Illustrated by Lorena Alvarez

"Happy birthday Tom!"
said Grandpa.

"Just what I wanted,"
Tom cried, "tin soldiers!"

"Oh dear! This soldier only has one leg," said Grandpa.

Tom didn't mind.
He spent all day playing.

At bedtime, he packed the soldiers back in their box.

But the one-legged soldier was missing.

"Where's he gone?"
wondered Tom.

"You can look for him
tomorrow," said Grandpa.

Tom's other toys waited until he was asleep.

Now it was their turn to play.
Whoopee!
Ha ha!
Yippee!

The soldiers tried to join in. But they were stuck in their box...

...except for the one-legged soldier.

He had fallen behind a pile of toy building blocks.

But he didn't join in the games.

He was gazing at the fairytale palace in the corner.

It once belonged to Tom's sister.

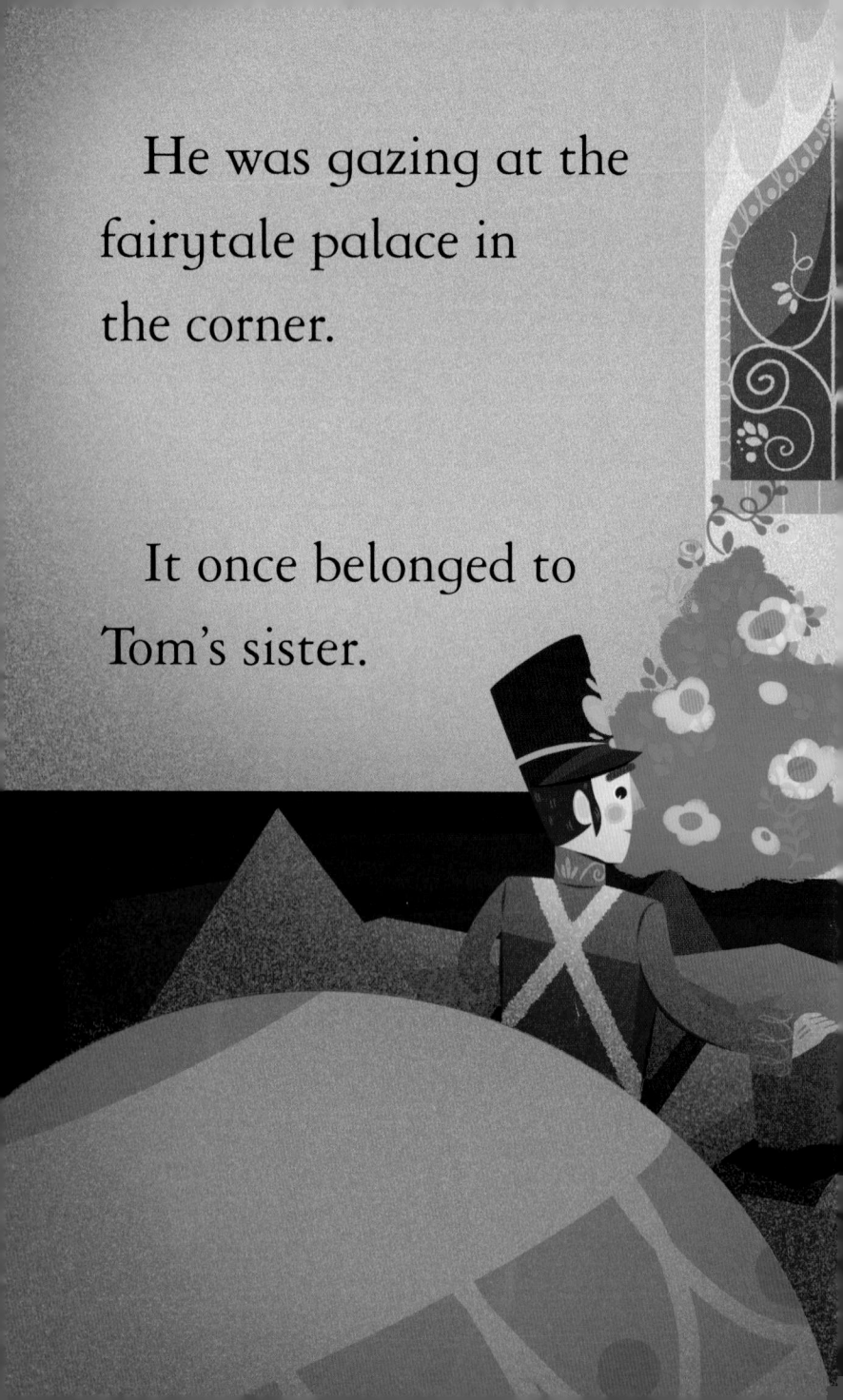

A paper ballerina doll
stood in the doorway.

The pretty ballerina was dancing on one leg.

"She'd be a perfect wife for me," said the soldier.

Suddenly, the grumpy jack-in-the-box sprang up.
Keep your eyes to yourself!

The soldier ignored him.
He smiled at the ballerina.

She smiled back.

The jealous jack-in-the-box turned bright red.

"Just wait," he fumed.

The next morning, Tom found his missing soldier.

He put him by the window.

The cruel jack-in-the-box saw his chance.

He took a deep breath, and blew as hard as he could.

The tin soldier fell
out of the window...

He landed...
Woooah!
...on the street below.

"Ow!" cried the soldier.

He tried to move. But his foot was stuck.

Two boys ran up.
"Look!" shouted one.
"A tin soldier."

"Let's turn him into a sailor," said the other.

They made a little boat out of an old newspaper.

They stood the tin soldier in the boat.

Then they dropped it in the gutter.

The soldier's boat sailed along the street.
Ha ha!
Oh no!

The tin soldier wished the boat would stop.
I feel sick.

But things were about to get worse.

There was a drain hole in the road ahead.

The paper boat shot down the drain.

It landed, splosh, in a dirty, smelly sewer.

"Pooh!" said the soldier, as he sailed along the tunnel.

He turned the bend. A fat black rat was in his way.

"Pay me a penny to pass!" ordered the rat.

The soldier had no money.
He couldn't stop anyway.

The soldier sailed on and on.

"Will I ever see the ballerina doll again?" he wondered.

Just then, he noticed daylight up ahead.

Seconds later, the boat whooshed out of the sewer.

It landed...
Woooah!
...in a river.

The tin soldier was glad to be out of the sewer.

But he wasn't happy for long. Now his boat was leaking.

The next moment, he was sinking like a stone.

And things were about to get worse.

A huge fish swam by.
Mmm, he looks tasty.

It swallowed the tin soldier in one gulp.

The soldier sat sadly in the fish's tummy.

But his luck was about to change.

A man caught the fish.

He took it to sell at the market.

Tom's Grandpa bought the fish.

He carried it home for supper.

He unwrapped the fish...

and the tin soldier fell out.

Grandpa took the tin soldier to Tom's room.

"Welcome home, soldier!" shouted Tom.

All the toys were glad
to see the tin soldier...
except one.
Grrrr!

He went hopping mad...

broke his spring...

and never worked again.

The very next day, the tin soldier married the lovely ballerina.

And they invited all the toys to a noisy party.

After Tom was asleep,
of course.
Whoopee!
Ha ha!
Yippee!

About the story

The Steadfast Tin Soldier was first written by Hans Christian Andersen in 1838. The original version had a very sad ending. The tin soldier and the paper ballerina melted in a fireplace. All that was left of them was a heart-shaped piece of tin and a black sequin.

Series editor: Lesley Sims

This edition first published in 2013 by Usborne Publishing Ltd., Usborne House, 83-85 Saffron Hill, London EC1N 8RT, England. www.usborne.com Copyright © 2013, 2012 Usborne Publishing Ltd.

All rights reserved. No part of this publication may be reproduced, stored in a retrieval system or transmitted in any form or by any means, electronic, mechanical, photocopying, recording or otherwise, without the prior permission of the publisher. The name Usborne and the devices are Trade Marks of Usborne Publishing Ltd.
UE. First published in America in 2013.